THIS WALKER BOOK BELONGS TO:

_____

_____

_____

_____

For
Elizabeth and Lucy

First published 1988 by Walker Books Ltd
87 Vauxhall Walk, London SE11 5HJ

This edition published 1989

© 1986 Blackbird Design Pty Ltd

Printed in Italy by Lito di Roberto Terrazzi

British Library Cataloguing in Publication Data
Graham, Bob
Has anyone here seen William?
I. Title
823'.914[J]   PZ7
ISBN 0-7445-1339-1

Has anyone here seen WILLIAM?

Bob Graham

WALKER BOOKS
LONDON

Nobody saw William's first step.

It was straight into mid-air. He rolled down the steps like
a soft red rubber ball – followed by his wind-up bear.

"Where's your brother, Jeremy? Ruth? Alice?"

The bear now walked with a slight limp and often fell over.
So did William. Things had to be moved out of his reach.
The handles of pots were turned in and the curtains tied up.

But William's mum and dad sometimes forgot.
"Did you tie the curtains in the children's room, dear?"

Now that William was walking, he was just like his bear.

Wind him up and off he would go.
Nothing stopped him until the key ran out.

His sisters and brother did not always watch him.

Sooner or later someone would say...

Has anyone here seen William?

On his second birthday, William went shopping for a new shirt.

His patched and rusty bear went walking. So did William.

Suddenly William was gone. His mum ran frantically into the street.

That afternoon, there was a party with a
special chocolate birthday cake for William.

"Keep a watch on William. He's been lost once
today already."

Long after the party was over and the children had
been tucked up in bed,

and the dog had been put in her basket in the kitchen,

and all were asleep,
there was a noise downstairs.

Slowly, the kitchen door swung open…

and there was William!
The key in his old bear had made its last turn.

William had stopped too... at least until tomorrow.

MORE WALKER PAPERBACKS

THE PRE-SCHOOL YEARS

John Satchwell
& Katy Sleight
Monster Maths
ODD ONE OUT   BIG AND LITTLE
COUNTING   SHAPES   ADD ONE   SORTING
WHAT TIME IS IT?   TAKE AWAY ONE

FOR THE VERY YOUNG

John Burningham
Concept books
COLOURS   ALPHABET
OPPOSITES   NUMBERS

Byron Barton
TRAINS   TRUCKS   BOATS   AEROPLANES

PICTURE BOOKS
For All Ages

Colin McNaughton
THERE'S AN AWFUL LOT OF WEIRDOS IN
OUR NEIGHBOURHOOD
SANTA CLAUS IS SUPERMAN

Russell Hoban
& Colin McNaughton
The Hungry Three
THEY CAME FROM AARGH!
THE GREAT FRUIT GUM ROBBERY

Jill Murphy
FIVE MINUTES' PEACE
ALL IN ONE PIECE

Bob Graham
THE RED WOOLLEN BLANKET
HAS ANYONE HERE SEEN WILLIAM?

Philippa Pearce
& John Lawrence
EMILY'S OWN ELEPHANT

David Lloyd
& Charlotte Voake
THE RIDICULOUS STORY OF
GAMMER GURTON'S NEEDLE

Nicola Bayley
Copycats
SPIDER CAT   PARROT CAT   CRAB CAT
POLAR BEAR CAT   ELEPHANT CAT

Peter Dallas-Smith
& Peter Cross
TROUBLE FOR TRUMPETS

Philippe Dupasquier
THE GREAT ESCAPE

Sally Scott
THE THREE WONDERFUL BEGGARS

Bamber Gascoigne
& Joseph Wright
AMAZING FACTS BOOKS 1 & 2

Martin Handford
WHERE'S WALLY?
WHERE'S WALLY NOW?